W9-BWJ-849

Rumpelstiltskin's Daughter

Diane Stanley

Morrow Junior Books
New York

❧ POSTCARD ❧

Dearest Mom + Dad,
Don't worry! I'm OK!!
But you'll never guess where
I am... here's a hint — mom
spent 2 nights here a
long, long time ago. If
it weren't for Dad, she
might still be here. And
Got it? Right!! And
you-know-who hasn't
changed a bit. But relax —
I have it all under
control. It's sort of an
adventure + if all works out,
there'll be some big changes soon!
More later and don't worry! Love xxx H.

Mr. and Mrs. R. Mackengeld
"The Cottage"
Wayfar, Kingdom
      003927

Gouache, colored pencil, and collage were used for the full-color illustrations.
The text type is 15.5-point Cheltenham.

Copyright © 1997 by Diane Stanley

Printed in the United States of America

1 3 5 7 9 10 8 6 4 2

Library of Congress Cataloging-in-Publication Data
Stanley, Diane.
Rumpelstiltskin's daughter / Diane Stanley.
p. cm.
Summary: Rumpelstiltskin's daughter may not be able
to spin straw into gold, but she is more than a match for a
monarch whose greed has blighted an entire kingdom.
ISBN 0-688-14327-X (trade)—ISBN 0-688-14328-8 (library)
[1. Fairy tales. 2. Greed—Fiction.] I. Title.
PZ7.S483Ru 1997 [E]—dc20 96-14834 CIP AC

For Meredith Charpentier—
wonderful editor, dear friend
lo these twenty years

Hi, Mom + Dad,
everything
is going like
clockwork—in fact, it's
almost too easy! Our
beloved ruler is about
as smart as a bunch of
asparagus. He has this
dog that yaps all the time
and these guards lurking
around everywhere, gnashing
their teeth and waving
their swords around. He
hides in here away from
the people 'cause they all
hate him for being so
greedy. But not for long—
look out for big changes!
I miss you. Your loving daughter, H.

POST CARD
FOR CORRESPONDENCE
FOR ADDRESS ONLY

Mr. + Mrs. R. Machengeld
"The Cottage"
Wayfar, Kingdom

003927

ONCE THERE WAS A MILLER'S DAUGHTER WHO got into a heap of trouble. It was all because her father liked to make up stories and pass them off as truth. Unfortunately, the story he told was that his daughter could spin straw into gold, which, of course, she could not. Even more unfortunately, he told this whopper in the hearing of a palace servant who rushed right off to tell the king. Since the king loved nothing in this world more than gold, he had the miller's daughter hauled up to the palace immediately and made her an offer she couldn't refuse. He put her in a room full of straw and ordered her to spin it into gold by morning, or die.

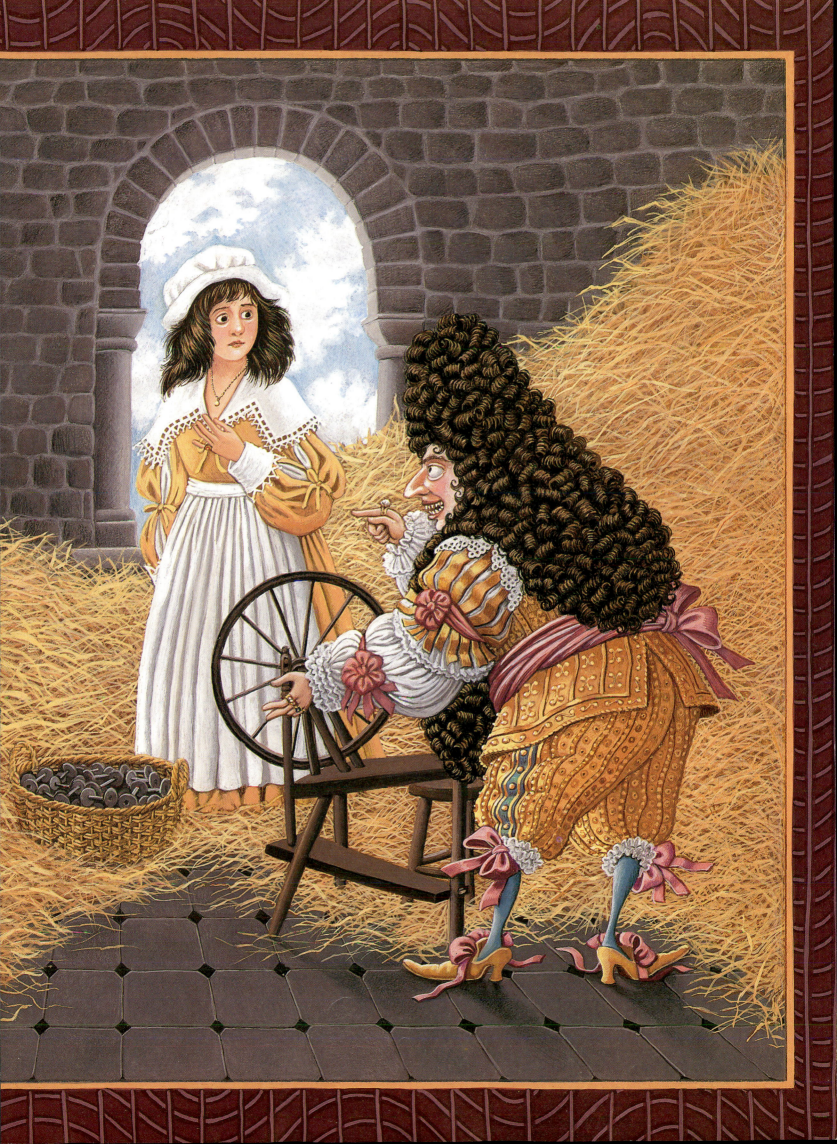

By one of those unlikely coincidences so common in fairy tales, no sooner had the king closed and bolted the door than a very small gentleman showed up and revealed that he really *could* spin straw into gold. Furthermore, he offered to do it in exchange for her necklace, which was made of gold-tone metal and wasn't worth ten cents. Naturally, she agreed.

The next morning, the king was so overjoyed with his room full of gold that he rewarded the miller's daughter by doubling the amount of straw and repeating his threat. Once again, Rumpelstiltskin (for that was his name) arrived to help her out. This time she gave him her cigar-band pinkie ring.

After this second success, the king was practically apoplectic with greed. He proceeded to empty every barn in the neighborhood of straw and to fill the room with it. This time, he added a little sugar to sweeten the pot: If she turned it all into gold, he would make her his queen. You can just imagine how the miller's daughter was feeling when Rumpelstiltskin popped in for the third time.

"That's quite a pile," he said. "I suppose you want me to spin it into gold."

"Well, the situation has changed just a bit," said the miller's daughter (who also had a name—it was Meredith). "If you *don't*, I will die. If you *do*, I marry the king."

Now *that*, thought Rumpelstiltskin, has possibilities. After all, getting to be the queen was a big step up for a miller's daughter. She would surely pay him anything. And there was only one thing in the world he really wanted—a little child to love and care for.

"Okay, here's the deal," he said. "I will spin the straw into gold, just like before. In return, once you become queen, you must let me adopt your firstborn child. I promise I'll be an excellent father. I know all the lullabies. I'll read to the child every day. I'll even coach Little League."

"You've got to be kidding," Meredith said. "I'd rather marry *you* than that jerk!"

"*Really?*" said Rumpelstiltskin, and he blushed all the way from the top of his head to the tip of his toes (which admittedly wasn't very far, because he was so short).

"Sure," she said. "I like your ideas on parenting, you'd make a good provider, and I have a weakness for short men."

So Rumpelstiltskin spun a golden ladder, and they escaped out the window. They were married the very next day and lived happily together far, far away from the palace.

Meredith and Rumpelstiltskin lived a quiet country life, raising chickens and growing vegetables. Every now and then, when they needed something they couldn't make or grow, Rumpelstiltskin would spin up a little gold to buy it with.

Now, they had a daughter, and she was just as sunny and clever as you would expect her to be, having such devoted parents. When she was sixteen, they decided she ought to see more of the world, so every now and then they allowed her to take the gold into town to exchange it for coins and to do a little shopping.

The goldsmith grew curious about the pretty country girl who came in with those odd coils of gold. He mentioned it to his friend the baker, who mentioned it to the blacksmith, who mentioned it to the tax collector, who hurried to the palace and told the king.

It may not surprise you to learn that the king hadn't changed a bit. If anything, he was greedier than before. As he listened, his eyes glittered. "I once knew a miller's daughter who could make gold like that," he said. "Unfortunately, she got away. Let's make sure *this* one doesn't."

So the next time Rumpelstiltskin's daughter went to see the gold-smith, two of the king's guards were waiting for her. In a red-hot minute, she was in a carriage and speeding toward the palace. And what she saw on the way broke her heart. Everywhere the fields lay barren. Sickly children stood begging beside the road. Nobody in the kingdom had anything anymore, because the king had it all.

Finally they reached the palace. There were high walls around it and a moat full of crocodiles. Armed guards were everywhere, gnashing their teeth, clutching their swords, and peering about with shifty eyes. As the carriage went over the bridge and under the portcullis, the hungry people shook their fists at them. It was not a pretty sight.

Rumpelstiltskin's daughter was taken at once to the grand chamber where the king sat on his golden throne. He didn't waste time on idle pleasantries.

"Where did you get *this*?" he asked, showing her the gold.

"Uh…," said Rumpelstiltskin's daughter.

"I thought so," said the king. "Guards, take her to the tower and see what she can do with all that straw."

Rumpelstiltskin's daughter looked around. She saw a pile of straw the size of a bus. She saw a locked door and high windows. She gave a big sigh and began to think. She knew her father could get her out of this pickle. But she had heard stories about the king all her life. One room full of gold would never satisfy him. Her father would be stuck here, spinning, until there was not an iota of straw left in the kingdom.

After a while she climbed the pile of straw and thought some more. She thought about the poor farmers and about the hungry children with their thin faces and sad eyes. She put the two thoughts together and cooked up a plan. Then Rumpelstiltskin's daughter curled up and went to sleep.

The next day, the king was very disappointed.

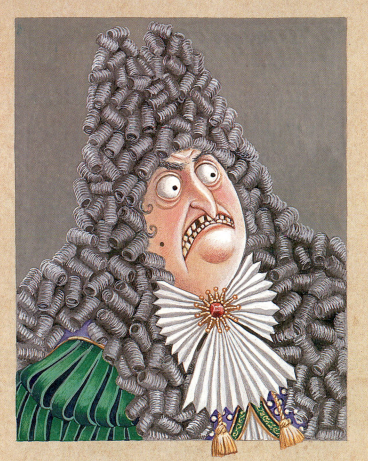

"Where's my gold?" he wanted to know.

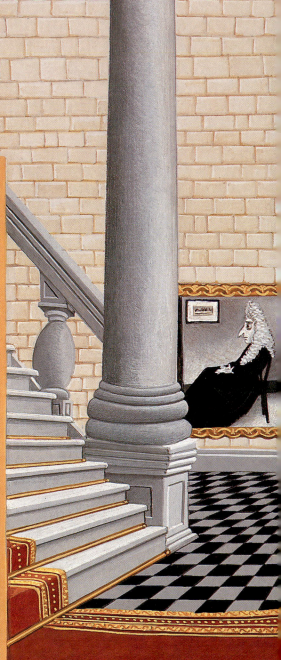

"I'm sure you have rooms full of it upstairs," said Rumpelstiltskin's daughter. And she was right. He did.

"But I want *more*!" he said. "And I want *you* to make it for me."

"Alas," she said, "I never made gold in my life. But"—and here she paused for effect—"I saw my grandfather make it." When the king's face brightened, she added, "He died years ago."

"Surely you remember how he did it," cried the king. "Think! Think!"

"Well," she said slowly, "there is one thing I'm sure of. He didn't spin it, he *grew* it."

The next morning the king and Rumpelstiltskin's daughter got into his glittering coach, with two guards up front and two guards behind and a huge bag of gold inside. They drove under the portcullis, over the bridge, and out into the countryside. At the first farm they came to, they stopped and sent for the farmer. He was thin and ragged and barefoot. So were his wife and children.

"Now tell the farmer he must plant this gold coin in his field, and you will come back in the fall to collect everything it has grown. Tell him you will give him another gold coin for his pains," she whispered.

"Do I *have* to?" the king whined.

"Well, I don't know," she said. "That's how my grandfather always did it."

"Okay," said the king. "But this better work." He gave the farmer two gold coins, and they hurried on to the next farm. By the end of the week they had covered the entire kingdom.

All through the summer the king was restless. "Is it time yet?" he would ask. "Is the gold ripe?"

"Wait," said Rumpelstiltskin's daughter.

Finally August came and went.

"Now," she said. "Now you can go and see what has grown in the fields."

So once again they piled into the glittering coach (with two guards up front and two guards behind) and brought along wagons to carry the gold and a lot more guards to protect it.

As they neared the first farm, the king gasped with joy. The field shone golden in the morning sun.

"Gold!" he cried.

"No," said Rumpelstiltskin's daughter, "something better than gold."

"How can anything be better than gold?" said the king.

"It's wheat," she said. "You can eat it. You can't eat gold."

Before the king could start turning purple, the farmer and his family came running toward the carriage. In their arms they carried baskets of wheat and barley and apples and green beans and pumpkins and corn and I don't know what all. They piled it into the wagon and kissed the king's hand, grinning ear to ear. I can promise you that nothing like that had ever happened to the king before.

"Well," he said sheepishly, "maybe there will be gold at the next place."

But everywhere it was the same. The land prospered, the children looked healthy, and the king was a hero. At the end of the week they returned to the palace with all the food the wagons could carry.

The cook was so overjoyed, he put on a sumptuous feast to celebrate. Unfortunately, there was no one to invite except Rumpelstiltskin's daughter and the guards, who spent the whole meal gnashing their teeth, clutching their swords, and peering about with shifty eyes.

"I wish they'd quit that," said Rumpelstiltskin's daughter.

After dinner, the king spoke. "That was all very nice, my dear," he said, "but you must have been mistaken. That was how your grandfather grew *food*, not how he made gold."

"Right," she said as she pulled her shawl tightly around her shoulders and gazed longingly at the fire. Even in the palace she could feel the chill of autumn. *Time for phase two*, she thought.

"Of course you're right," she said. "I told you it was long ago. But I think I remember now. He didn't grow gold. He *knitted* it with golden knitting needles."

So the next day they loaded the coach with knitting needles, a bag of gold, and lots and lots of yellow wool. Then they headed off under the portcullis, over the bridge (with two guards up front and two guards behind), and out into the countryside.

At the first cottage they came to, they asked to see the granny. She hobbled to the door in her rags and curtsied to the king.

"Now," whispered Rumpelstiltskin's daughter, "give her a bag of wool and a pair of needles. Tell her to knit it all up and you will come back in a month to collect your riches. Give her a gold coin for her pains."

"Do I *have* to?" the king whined.

"My grandfather always did," she said. "I would, if I were you."

And so they went all over the kingdom, hiring every granny they could find.

At the end of the month, the king ordered his coach and wagons, rounded up his guards, and went to see the grannies. As he neared the first cottage, he heard the sound of singing. Looking out the window, the king saw crowds of happy villagers waiting there to greet him, cheering wildly as he passed. And every one of them was warm as toast in yellow woolly clothes.

"Gold!" cried the king.

"Something better than gold," said Rumpelstiltskin's daughter. "Your people will be warm all winter."

Everyone brought presents for the king. By the time he got back to his palace, he had seventeen sweaters, forty-two mufflers, eight vests, one pair of knickers, one hundred and thirty-five pairs of socks, twelve nightcaps, and a tam-o'-shanter. All the color of gold.

"Do they suit me?" asked the king as he tried them on.
"Absolutely," said Rumpelstiltskin's daughter.

The guards just stood there, gnashing their teeth, clutching their swords, and peering about with shifty eyes.

"Don't you think it's time you got rid of them?" she suggested. "And the walls and the moat and the crocodiles, too. You don't need them anymore—your people love you now."

She was right, as always, so the king set the guards to work tearing down the walls. And with the stones, they built a zoo for the crocodiles and houses for the poor.

"Are you sure you don't remember how your grandfather made gold?" asked the king one day.

"I'm afraid not," she said.

"It's a terrible pity," he sighed. "But you did try. And as a reward, I have decided to make you my queen."

"Why don't you make me prime minister instead," suggested Rumpelstiltskin's daughter.

And so the king did just that. He built her a nice house near the palace, and once a month she took time off to visit her parents. The people of the kingdom never went cold or hungry again. And whenever the king started worrying about gold, she sent him on a goodwill tour throughout the countryside, which cheered him right up.

Oh, and I forgot to tell you—Rumpelstiltskin's daughter had a name, too. It was Hope.